A Thousand Pails of Water

by Ronald Roy
pictures by Vo-Dinh Mai

Alfred A. Knopf   New York

This is a Borzoi Book published by Alfred A. Knopf, Inc. Text Copyright © 1978 by Ronald Roy. Illustrations Copyright © 1978 by Vo-Dinh Mai. All rights reserved under International and Pan-American Copyright Conventions. Published in the United States by Alfred A. Knopf, a division of Random House, Inc., New York, and simultaneously in Canada by Random House of Canada Limited, Toronto. Manufactured in the United States of America. Library of Congress Cataloging in Publication Data. Roy, Ronald, 1940-   A thousand pails of water. Summary: A small boy's infectious determination saves the life of a whale beached near an oriental whaling village.   [1. Whales—Fiction] I. Vo-Dinh Mai.   II. Title. PZ7.R8139Th   [E]   78-3275   ISBN 0-394-83752-5   ISBN 0-394-93752-X lib bdg.   First Edition   10 9 8 7 6 5 4 3 2 1

For Robin, who knew,
with affection

Yukio lived in a village where people fished and hunted whales to make their living. Yukio's father, too, was a whale hunter.

"Why do you kill the whales, Father?" Yukio asked. "Suki's father works in the market and his hands are never red from blood."

"Hunting the whale is all I know," his father answered.

But Yukio did not understand.

Yukio went to his grandfather and asked again. "Why does my father kill the whales?"

"Your father does what he must do," his grandfather said. "Let him be, little one, and ask your questions of the sea."

So Yukio went to the sea.

Small creatures scurried from under his feet in the tide pools. Large scavenger birds screamed at him from the sky, "Bring us food!"

Then Yukio saw a whale that had be-
come lodged between some rocks and was
left behind when the tide went out.

The large tail flukes beat the sand,
helplessly. The eye, as big as Yukio's hand,
rolled in fright.

Yukio knew that the whale would not
live long out of the sea.

"I will help you, sir," he said.

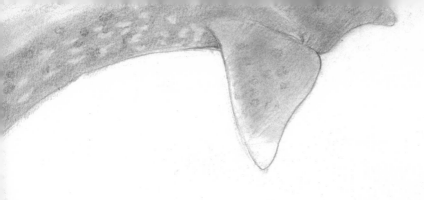

But how? The whale was huge, like a temple.

Yukio raced to the water's edge. Was the tide coming in or going out? In, he decided, by the way the little fingers of foam climbed higher with each new wave.

The sun was hot on Yukio's back as he stood looking at the whale.

Yukio filled his pail with water and threw it over the great head.

"You are so big and my pail is so small!" he cried. "But I will throw a thousand pails of water over you before I stop."

The second pail went on the head as well, and the third and the fourth. But Yukio knew he must wet every part of the whale or it would die in the sun.

Yukio made many trips to the sea for water, counting as he went. He threw four pails on the body, then four on the tail, and then three on the head.

There was a little shade on one side of the big gray prisoner. Yukio sat there, out of breath, his heart pounding. Then he looked in the whale's eye and remembered his promise.

Yukio went back to the sea and stooped to fill his pail. How many had he filled so far? He had lost count. But he knew he must not stop.

Yukio fell, the precious water spilling from his pail. He cried, and his tears disappeared into the sand.

A wave touched his foot, as if to say, "Get up and carry more water. I am coming, but I am very slow."

Yukio filled his pail over and over. His back hurt, and his arms—but he threw and threw.

He fell again, but this time he did not get up.

Yukio felt himself being lifted.

"You have worked hard, little one. Now let us help."

Yukio's grandfather lay him in the shade of one of the rocks. Yukio watched his grandfather throw his first pail of water and go for another.

"Hurry!" Yukio wanted to scream, for his grandfather was old and walked slowly.

Then Yukio heard the voices. His father and the village people were running toward the sea. They carried pails and buckets and anything that would hold water.

Some of the villagers removed their jackets and soaked them in the sea. These they placed on the whale's burning skin. Soon the whale was wet all over.

Slowly the sea came closer and closer. At last it covered the huge tail. The village people ran back and forth carrying water, shouting to each other. Yukio knew the whale would be saved.

Yukio's father came and stood by him. "Thank you, Father," Yukio said, "for bringing the village people to help."

"You are strong and good," his father said. "But to save a whale many hands must carry the water."

Now the whale was moving with each new wave. Suddenly a great one lifted him free of the rocks. He was still for a moment, then, with a flip of his tail, swam out to sea.

The villagers watched silently, as the whale swam farther and farther from their shore. Then they turned and walked toward the village.

Except for Yukio, who was asleep in the arms of his father.

He had carried a thousand pails of water, and he was tired.

Ronald Roy, a sixth grade teacher, has long been interested in children and children's books. Though he has only recently begun writing, three of his stories are scheduled for publication. An ardent conservationist and avid traveler, Mr. Roy and his wife Robin live in Hartford, Connecticut.

Vo-Dinh Mai is a well-known painter and printmaker. He has illustrated many books including *The Magic Drum*, a Japanese folktale for children, and the Christopher Award-winning *First Snow*, written by his wife Helen Coutant. They live with their two daughters in Burkittsville, Maryland.